P9-CFC-213

LEBANON VALLEY COLLEGE LIBRARY

You can find these animals on the inside covers

1	Marsupial mouse	13	Possum
2	Koala	14	Grandma
3	Cassowary	15	Pelican
4	Frill-necked lizard	16	Echidna
5	Dingo	17	Emu
6	Platypus	18	Eastern rosella
7	Galah	19	Kookaburra
8	Wedge-tailed eagle	20	Lyrebird
9	Rabbit-eared bandicoot	21	Children's python
10	Red kangaroo	22	Goanna
11	Silver gull	23	Marsupial mouse (another one)
12	Wombat		

Copyright © 1983 Graeme Base

Published in 1990 by Harry N. Abrams, Incorporated, New York

First published in Australia in 1983 by Thomas Nelson Australia

All rights reserved. No part of the contents of this book may be reproduced without the written permission of the publishers

Printed and bound in China

ISBN 0-8109-1547-2
Library of Congress Catalog Card Number: 90-81758

Reprinted 2004
10 9 8 7 6

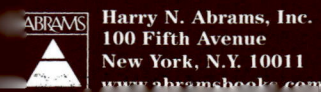
Harry N. Abrams, Inc.
100 Fifth Avenue
New York, N.Y. 10011
www.abramsbooks.com

Abrams is a subsidiary of

LA MARTINIÈRE

My Grandma lived in GOOLIGULCH

Graeme Base

Harry N. Abrams, Inc., Publishers, New York

LEBANON VALLEY COLLEGE LIBRARY

My Grandma lived in Gooligulch,
  Near Bandywallop East,
A fair way north of Murrumbum
  (Five hundred miles at least).

A little west of Lawson's Rest,
  And south of Johnson's Gap,
But nowhere much near anywhere
  That shows up on the map.

Now Gooligulch has got a pub,
  A mainstreet with a hall,
A petrol pump that doesn't work –
  And not much else at all.

Except for Grandma; dear old Gran,
  And this I say with pride,
For Gran it was that made old Gooli'
  Famous far and wide.

In Sydney and in Melbourne Town,
　　They all knew Grandma's name,
And all about the animals,
　　That Grandma used to tame.

And if a stranger came to town,
　　(Perhaps just passing through),
He'd see my Grandma riding by,
　　Atop a kangaroo.

Or sometimes in a two-wheeled gig,
　　A wombat at the bit,
And next to Grandma in the back,
　　A bandicoot would sit.

The townsfolk thought it very odd,
　　But Grandma took no heed.
She said that she enjoyed the view,
　　Upon her hopping steed.

And as for training wombats, well,
　　It took no time at all,
To teach them how to pull a gig,
　　And come and go at call.

Now Grandma lived just out of town,
 A mile beyond the pub,
Down by a little billabong,
 That nestled in the scrub.

Upon a hillside, ringed with trees,
 Her rambling 'mansion' stood –
A jumbled maze of tin and canvas,
 Bits of string and wood.

And from a window out the back,
 She'd sit and watch galahs,
Fly down beside the pool and drink,
 Beneath the evening stars.

In years gone by the house was full
    Of birds both big and small.
Rosellas, eagles, coots and magpies,
    Roosting in the hall.

While in the tiny living-room
    An old goanna sat,
And played a game of two-up,
    With a dingo and a rat.

My Grandma whiled the hours away,
    Conversing with a coot,
Or listening to the wombat,
    Play a tune upon his lute.

There was a time, the locals say,
When emus came to dine,
And stood about all evening,
Drinking eucalyptus wine.

They dressed for the occasion,
(Looking rather out of date),
And were spreading idle gossip,
In a less than sober state.

But then a frill-necked lizard,
Gave one ancient bird a scare,
And the dinner guests all panicked,
Running madly here and there.

Some kookaburras heard the noise,
And came to watch the show,
And laughed so much that
Grandma sternly told them all to go.

By the time the fuss was over,
There was not a guest in sight,
But then that's the way with emus –
Grandma said they're not too bright.

One year when it was very hot,
  Old Grandma went away,
And took the wombat with her,
  On a seaside holiday.

She didn't go by elephant,
  Or on a polar bear,
(Besides, you ought to know,
  You don't find elephants up there).

She didn't own a camel,
  And they cost too much to buy,
So Grandma bought some goggles,
  And decided she would fly.

The eagle wouldn't take them,
  And the coot was far too weak,
But a pelican consented,
  So they climbed into its beak.

And off they flew, quite low at first,
  Then climbing very high,
And as they turned towards the sea,
  The wombat waved goodbye.

They flew across the desert sands,
  And over mountains too,
Until at dusk they reached a place,
  Where giant tree-ferns grew.

The pelican came gliding down,
  To land beside a creek,
And Grandma and the wombat,
  Climbed down gladly from its beak.

Then while the pelican relaxed,
  And Grandma cooked the tea,
The wombat wandered down the creek,
  To see what he could see.

The trees were full of creatures,
  With unfriendly, glowing eyes,
And giant furry spiders hunted
  Giant furry flies.

A baby tree-snake slithered by,
  And gave him such a start,
That poor old wombat turned and fled,
  With terror in his heart.

And so they spent the night there,
  But the wombat stayed awake,
Looking nervously around him
  For a wombat-eating snake.

When morning came they journeyed on,
      And reached the sea at last.
The rolling waves came crashing in —
      The tide was running fast.

But undeterred my Grandma donned
      Her frilly bathing gear,
And dived into the foaming surf,
      Without a trace of fear.

She sat upon her blow-up horse,
      While wombat went to sleep.
The pelican went fishing,
      Where the sea was not so deep.

But when the wombat woke,
      The tide had carried her away. . .
And no-one's seen my Grandma,
      Even to this very day.

And yet, I have a feeling,
 That my Grandma's still alive,
Having drifted to an island,
 Where she'd manage to survive.

From there perhaps she made her way,
 To England or to Spain,
Or maybe San Francisco,
 On a Western Railway train.

She could be taming tigers,
 In the jungles of Tingoor...

...But *I* think she's back in Gooligulch,
Just like before.